The Boy

By Rayne Havok

Rights

This is for all you sickos out there.

And of course, B, who stands by me while I write disgusting and offensive things and still knows I'm a sweet girl.

Summary

Chop has that familiar craving, the one that makes him itch; drives him crazy until he gets his release.

Join him tonight as he invites himself into a friendly neighborhood home and indulges himself in all that is not offered.

Warning:

I am told this should have an 'extreme' warning.

Because these things are always in my head and on my mind, I don't always consider them to be over-the-top. To some it may be run-of-the mill and to others it may be too much.

If you feel like you may have issues reading 'extreme' stories, please don't bother with this one, you may be offended.

This story has many graphic scenes of rape some may find offensive, please remember that this is a work of fiction.

Chapter one

Chop

Hey, Chop, you leavin' man?" Gabe, the fucking idiot who loves to follow me around asks.

"Yea, got shit I gotta do."

I don't have anything in particular that I really have to get away for. But I can't be here another second. My skin is crawling; itching to leave.

The bar is usually my second home– the place I come to escape. The shady dump with dim lights and sticky floors has been my hunting ground and home away from home for a long time now. Tonight, I need something else.

I give my card to the bartender, Jenn– a hot little red head who's down to fuck most nights. Settling my tab, I head for the door.

Gabe stops me again.

Fucker.

"Cha need?" I say when he grabs for my elbow. All my self- control teetering toward punching him in the face.

"Just wondering if you heard from Jamie?"

Fucking Jamie.

The bitch that he's been after forever. She's had a thing for me and wouldn't leave me alone, no matter how shitty I treated her.

"Nah, man, I ain't seen 'er." I say it in a way that makes that the end of the conversation. I leave before I have to do something painful to him for holding me up.

It's late, the only people on the street are drunkards trying to find their ways home. I have steam to blow off and I've had too much to drink to get on my bike without alerting law enforcement to my predicament. So, I hoof it; not really heading home directly– got too much going on in my head for such a short walk to be enough.

It's dark, save for the outdated street lights with yellowing bulbs doing nothing to help you see inside the shadows of the darkened alleys, here more for the aesthetic look of them.

One of the ladies on the street catches my eye, she's alone and stumbling in her heels. The skirt she's wearing is hiked up and the bottom of her ass is hanging out. It's a nice round ass, I can see her black laced thong stuck inside the crack.

I follow behind her for a while; she doesn't seem fazed by me. She stumbles and falls to her knees, her arms catch her before she face plants. I come to her aid, reaching out a hand for her to take.

Once she has made it back to her feet she reacts to seeing me for the first time and the telltale look in her eyes says she wants me. She bites her lip and gives me her best impression of 'fuck me' eyes I've seen in a long time. I can smell the alcohol and desperation on her.

If I was in the mood for something consensual I'd be all over this chick. Her long blond hair and blue eyes are usually what I like. Her hot little body and barely- there clothes would get any man in the mood. Not for me... not tonight.

"Hi." She smiles.

"You ok now?" I ask.

"I think so." She surveys her body with her hands, one of which has a small cut on the palm and she smears it across her chest without realizing it. I almost change my mind.

Almost.

"You better get home then."

"You want to follow me? Make sure I get home safe?"

I read the message between the lines. "You got this, girl." I smack her now fully- exposed ass harder than I intended, the sound of it echoing through the night, and start walking again.

I hear her huff, but I don't turn. I'm even more irritated now than I was when I left the bar. I hate nights like this, the nights I can't stop thinking about it–the thing that lives inside of me.

I walk faster, picking up speed; trying to outrun the swirling thoughts fighting for attention in my head. I can't fucking do this. I can't get rid of the itch, though. It grows until I have to listen– until I have to follow its orders. Don't get me wrong, I love that little demon that lurks inside of me, but it has been getting more demanding and leaving me with not much else to think about.

I'm sure I could have made that girl *not* want me after we got into it, I could scare her into a fight; maybe she'd even like to play like that. I think about going back to find her, but I don't. Something inside me knows it's not going to be enough.

Fuck.

I wander into a neighborhood; completely lost in a fantasy of everything I need– all the fucked up things that I crave. Sometimes it helps to live in the past– to revel in the memories. I feel it strongly in my bones. The need.

Looking around for something to get my mind settled, a distraction from the urge. My eyes land on a window, the vertical blinds are open. My breath catches, exciting me more than calming me. I get that feeling deep inside me, the feeling I spend most of my time shoving down, knowing I can't encourage it. It hits me like a brick in the gut.

I can see straight through the house, a long room that starts with a living area and opens into a dining room. From here, I can see six adults, three women and three men, seemingly coupled up and three teenaged kids. They are a good looking group of people, so happy and unassuming. Middle class house and the people in there seem to fit the stereotype of what would be found inside.

They're drinking wine, something trendy, I'm sure. The kids are grouped together on the large sectional sofa away from the adults on their phones. As close as kids these days come to social interaction.

Walking across the manicured lawn, I get closer to the glass, standing inches from it. No one is paying any attention to me and the darkness that comes from having no street lights is giving me perfect refuge.

I watch as conversation flows between the people around the table. Laughing and enjoying life. I catch sight of one of the women in particular, uptight and snobby looking. My favorite– if I had to choose. I would love to break her down and show her who the fuck is really in charge. Break her to the point of tears, begging for me to stop. Deep down, knowing I won't. Women like her always so on top of their social circles, vying for queen bee. I love to rip that illusion away from them.

My cock stirs.

This woman is perfect. I can tell she is leading the conversation, everyone angled toward her. She commands the room.

I reach my hand into the front of my pants and squeeze my aching cock. Giving a quick look around the street before finding her in the room again. I don't want to come right now. I love the need that comes from being right on the edge of not finishing, stopping just before I explode. Instant gratification has never been my 'thing', I love the chase of it. The need that I feel going after that high, not wanting it to be over too soon.

My mouth is dry, I can't hear anything over my heavy breathing, coming faster as I pump my cock. I pull my hand away just as I feel the end near. I swallow what saliva I have to wet my throat and reach for the back of my pants, patting the waistband where I keep my gun.

This has to happen. I need this right now.

I watch a few minutes longer to see if anyone else may appear from somewhere else in the house. Nothing happens so I head for the door.

I settle for the 'my truck broke down' approach as I ring the doorbell. I hear a woman call "coming" just before the door opens.

It's her– the one that enticed my cock. My eyes go right to her full tits, but I'm able to pull them up to where it's more acceptable before she notices.

"Don't mean to interrupt you, ma'am." I give my best attempt at 'friendly guy who needs help'. "My truck just crapped out on me. Cell phones dead." I hold mine up; using it as a prop in my lie.

"Oh, um." She seems confused as to what I would need from her in this instance, worrying her bottom lip. I almost snatch her out of her house right then. I stop myself before I do, my hands itching to touch her.

"Is there a phone I can use? Out here, of course." I add when a panic comes into her eyes.

"Um… yeah, I think I can do that." She closes the door tightly after going inside, coming back in a flash.

She steps out onto the porch and shuts the door behind her, putting her less than a foot from me. I can smell her perfume; something sweet and heady. She hands me the phone as a second thought.

Her eyes take me in. I am gruff looking, dark hair, green eyes and about 6'4''. To this woman I may seem like a giant, probably no more than five feet herself. Petite and obviously into yoga or some other sort of body toning bullshit. Shoulder length, wildly curly blonde– with a hint of strawberry hair and the prettiest whiskey colored eyes, looking up into mine, softening a little as she sees nothing in mine to worry about. I definitely don't look like the monster that hides inside of me.

She seems to release the rest of her tension after I take the phone and put it to my ear after adding numbers into the keypad.

I watch her watch me. I've sobered completely, the adrenaline pushing the alcohol from my veins, she looks away self- consciously whenever our eyes meet– which is frequently because I've not stopped and she keeps returning to mine time and again.

I mumble some bullshit into the phone about needing a lift and hit end on it before handing it back to her. Her hand missing it when her eyes refuse to look away from mine to pay attention to the device.

I can't help but tease her, when her hand finally stumbles its connection with the phone, I don't let go on my end. She pulls harder. I let go finally with a half- sided smirk on my face. Something registers in her eyes, close to confusion. She turns quickly toward the door. I grab her hand before it reaches the knob.

"What's your name?" I ask, my tone in any other instance would be considered flirting. She seems to know that, squinting at me to try and calculate how to respond.

"Amy?" she says it like a question. Pulling her hand out of mine harder than it needed to be done; her elbow hitting the door with a thud. She hisses in pain, which only adds to this shit I have going on with me. I love seeing her grab her elbow and baby it. It goes against everything a normal person feels when watching someone hurting, I actually enjoy it. It looks so fucking good on her. Her brow scrunching and the sharp hiss she makes could be confused with the sound she would make while fucking.

"You ok?"

She nods, shaking her arm to rid her funny bone of the pain. "I should get inside."

She turns to the door again.

"What are you doing tonight?" I ask just before the door flies open. The man who had brought on this distraction is tall, only a few inches or so shorter than me. His frame is thin and tapered, where mine is thick and muscular– hours spent at the gym burning off the intense energy I often feel.

I reach my arm toward him in a gesture meant to be accepted with a shake. "I'm Chop." I tell him.

He looks at Amy, trying to gauge her feelings about this and he must not see anything alarming in her eyes because he shakes my hand; harder than necessary– to show me he isn't soft.

"Dan," he says flatly.

"You get everything taken care of, babe?" he wraps his arm around her waist, marking his territory.

My cheek twitches as I fight the laugh that begs to be heard. I could knock this fucker out in one hit without using my full strength and he wants to enter a pissing contest with me. I almost hope he tries something tonight. I'm usually more of a fucker than a fighter, but anything that gets the blood pumping is good for me.

Ok.

I move quicker than either of them can stop me and the gun is leveled at his temple. Amy is who I want my eyes on– to see her reaction to this, but mine stay trained on Dan. His eyes are a cartoon version of shock.

Dumb fuck.

I do laugh now, his face is too comical to not. "Let's take this inside– wouldn't want the neighbors to think something strange is going on."

They do, walking in front of me. Amy stumbles over the threshold and I catch her sore elbow in my hand before she can spill over. My fingers envelope her whole bicep, which is muscular but thin. She yelps when I dig my fingernails into her flesh.

I think of a few ways I could use this woman. I'd fucking break her in half if I went at her the way I'd really like to, maybe I'll get a chance tonight. I could very well make sure to leave enough time for it.

I fling her arm away from me, propelling her forward. The room falls quiet as everyone realizes what is happening. A quick count tells me that everyone is here and accounted for. I tell them all not to move. No one seems to have thought that they might have anyway. Shocked, as a collective whole, is all I read in them.

It's a nice neighborhood, things like this aren't supposed to happen here, thusly, making people like them unable to function when it finally does. I thank the 'false sense of security' gods as I give them further instructions.

"Everyone to the table. Phones right here." I point to the floor in the middle of the two groups. Hands start reaching around for devices. The clattering of them hitting the floor happens quickly after.

I nudge this fuck- face forward with the barrel of the gun. I can see the defiance in his eyes, but he is not crazy enough to try anything. *Yet*.

Amy stays close by his side, probably feeling a sense of protection toward him– like she could do anything about it if I pulled the trigger. I think I'll test that loyalty tonight.

Everyone has made it to the chairs around the rectangle table, scooting close together to keep their backs from facing me; choosing to butt against the wall instead. I tell these two to get there now as well.

The fear is evident on everyone, although the questions they have go unasked.

I take a minute to collect my thoughts– how this is going to go down tonight. I look around the neatly decorated, but mostly feminine room.

"Ok, so, this is what we're going to do." My voice is loud and commanding in the space, startling them. "I want to play a little. Nothing too horrible will happen tonight if you all can just follow directions. Think you can do that?" It is not true most of the time, and definitely not on a night like tonight where the little demon wants to play, but if I told them the truth it would be anarchy.

Silence. "I think I asked a fucking question. Do you all think you could follow some simple instructions if your lives depended on it? Because you fuckers can't even answer a simple fucking question."

Losing my cool really loosened their vocal cords; this time I get a mixture of nods and verbal confirmations. "That's better. Now, whose house is this?"

Amy answers that it is hers.

"Who else lives here?"

"Just Travis and me."

I look toward the man who came to her aid outside. "You Travis?"

He just shakes his head, offering me no more information.

"Ok… then who the fuck is Travis?" My voice is showing my irritation by progressively getting louder.

"I am," one of the teenagers who was sitting on the couch earlier says. Blond kid with shaggy hair, tallish for his age and trim. I can see it now, he has her rare colored eyes.

"You her kid?"

"Yea," he says.

"Who are your parents?" I ask the other two kids.

They both point to the same set of people– the youngest looking couple of the group.

"So, you don't have kids here?" I ask the last couple.

They shake their heads. His fat chins jiggling back and forth with the rapid movement. He is much older looking than her, who looks at least ten years his junior, bleach blonde, big tits. She looks like a trophy wife, probably the reason that there are no children between the two of them.

"My name is Chop, and now that we've all been so nicely introduced, let's fucking do this."

The expressions on their faces encourage me, fear of the unknown written everywhere. I love this part– the part that lets them all in on their fates. "I'm going to ask you, Amy, to please come here– stand right here." I point to the spot right next to me.

She takes a deep breath before standing and making her way over. I pull her closer to me, wrapping my arm around her shoulders. She stiffens but doesn't pull away. The man she is with– her boyfriend I assume, seethes.

"So, Amy, which of these fine people would you be least likely to miss if something were to happen to them?"

"What? You said if we followed your instructions no one would get hurt." She's panicking, pulling against my restraining hold.

"Well, sometimes people have to show that they mean business. I'm merely trying to show you I'm serious. It could be a hypothetical question, maybe nothing will happen to this person. I mean, it seems unlikely, but it *could* be the case. Either way, I'll need that fucking answer from you or I'll have to choose and you won't like the choice *I* make, I'll be sure of it." I give her a cocky smirk.

She holds her pleading eyes to mine. She must see what needs to be seen in them to make her choice because she swallows hard and says, "Stephen."

I know who Stephen is right away. It is him who jumps from the table, toppling over his chair. "Amy!" he shouts at her, the accusation thick in his voice. He tries to scramble away, but there isn't enough room for his large body to move quickly.

The polo shirt tucked tightly into his khaki pants makes me hate him instantly. I level the gun to him, "Come over here, Stephen."

He looks ready to hyperventilate.

"Would you rather do it yourself, or should I?"

"Please, you don't have to do this." He is shaking with fear, his legs nearly buckle as he reaches the spot on the floor I indicate for him to stop.

"I know, but I *want* to." I pull the trigger and half his face explodes, landing with an oof as his lungs empty of air when his body falls hard onto the floor.

Amy escapes my grasp, but only to slide down my body to the ground, her legs giving out.

The gasping and screaming that fills the air is from multiple sources– sounding together it is almost comedic. His wife doesn't do anything overboard, like I usually see, she simply looks at his dead body, tears rolling from her eyes. This furthers my idea that she is a trophy wife, a marriage of convenience and money, possibly.

I catch Travis in the corner of my eye, he is unaffected by the gruesome scene. The only one in the room who hadn't responded to the violence. I watch him until his eyes meet mine.

He doesn't look away. *Hmmm.*

Chapter two

Travis

I watch as this big fucking dude put a bullet into Stephen's face. Something I wish I could have done a thousand times. His wife is always over here bitching about all the horrible things he does to her. (All the things that *I* want to do to her)

She tells my mom she hates fucking him because he is so mean about it. He essentially rapes her whenever he wants to. I stay close by when she visits to hear all the details, fantasizing it would be me one day to force her into doing whatever the fuck I want to do to her. I jack off to that thought more often than not. Even now, as she is crying over him, all I can think about is how her tits are heaving as she cries.

Chapter Three

Chop

I pull the fat fucks body out of the way, leaving behind a smear of him along the floor.

"Ok, now everyone knows I mean business. Amy, thank you for helping out on that one."

Her response is almost a hiss. "Fuck you." She scrambles back to her seat, dragging her knees through the mess.

The words hit me in the dick. "I wouldn't talk like that to me, I already have my eye on you. I like a lady with a nasty mouth."

This seems to alarm her, but she snaps her mouth shut.

"Ok, now that that is out of the bag. You," I point to the man who is with the lady that didn't just witness hers husbands brains burst open. He is in good shape, on the shorter side but looks like he may be able to handle himself against a man of equal stature. "This is going to sound like a strange request. But, you know after someone loses someone dear to them they need a little companionship."

His wide eyes tell me he may know where I'm going with this.

"Don't you think Miss Trophy Wife over there looks so lonely after Mr. Fat Fuck lost his head?"

He shakes his head wildly.

His lady, and mother to two of the children looking on, looks horrified herself. "In case it's not clear, I'd like you to fuck her."

"I... I can't do that."

The boy, Travis, seems a little pissed now. I wonder where that's coming from.

"Travis."

He looks at me, lifting his eyebrows in response to his name being called.

"What's got you all pissy now? You want a chance with one of these girls?"

He looks away finally.

"Which one?" I ask.

His eyes meet mine for the briefest second before looking down again.

"You a virgin?"

His face turns red as confirmation.

"Which one you want? This one?" I walk over to the girl looking to be about his age and pull her up by her hair. She screams from the pain.

I watch closely and see his eyes subconsciously shoot to the trophy wife. I drop the girl back into her chair, being of no further use to me right now. I go to where his eyes were drawn. "You want this one?"

His tongue licks his lips before he looks up at me through his eyebrows.

I might actually like this kid. "Come 'er." He stands quicker than is polite for what I'm about to ask of him. I hold back a laugh.

I tell trophy wife to get undressed and lie down on the couch. She does it without being asked twice, going into auto- pilot and looking a little shaken by the whole experience. The task is quick, she was wearing a sundress with no bra and a strip of fabric as panties.

I can see what the boy sees in her, her large fake tits are perfect and her tiny waist with wide hips make her look even better naked. I almost think about giving her a go myself, but the thought of tearing Amy apart later holds me back.

"Alright, boy, go on over there and give it to her." I shove him a little, although he doesn't really need the extra push. I do it more for his sake– to give it the illusion the he's not so ready for this. I don't know why I feel the need to protect his perversion, but I do.

"I can't," he says once he's standing in front of her. The bulge in his pants says quite the opposite.

"You gonna need help? You want the girl to get you ready?"

He shakes his head before I can go collect her.

"You want me to bring your mom over there for you? Make her get on her knees for you?"

He looks at me; the thing that flashes in his eyes is not one of disgust.

"We may have a thing for the same woman." I can't really blame the kid, all those hormones and a hot as fuck mom has got to be confusing.

He looks panicked, so, I let up on him.

"Alright then, get started. Take your clothes off. Better yet, why don't you undress him?" I tell miss trophy. "His dick isn't going to suck itself– open up wide for him."

When she doesn't move I pull her up from her prone position by her hair and force her face into his crotch. "I told you to do something. You want to end up like the fat man?"

She shakes her head and moves her trembling hands to his zipper. I see the boy take a shaky breath and swallow hard.

"You ever had a blow job?" I ask him.

"No." His voice cracks.

Amy, his mom, shouts at me to stop, to leave him alone. I let her outburst go, this time– enjoying this shit too much to take my attention away from it.

Once his cock is out, harder than men my age get anymore, I push her forward until she is forced to open her lips. I watch as she moves him in and out of her mouth. She's pretty good at it, too. She takes him deep.

"You want in that pussy, boy?"

His eyes close, so I let him enjoy himself.

I reach between her legs. "Spread."

She does, moving the two inches I need to fit my hand between her naked thighs.

I put my fingers inside of her smooth pussy– easily as she seems to be wet. The fucking slut could be getting off on this.

"You like him, huh?" I fuck her quickly with two fingers, her pussy clamping down on them, squeezing tightly.

"You're gonna want to get in this, boy." I slap the mound of her pussy. She whines, but doesn't let up on him, the slurping sounds remain in perfect rhythm.

He looks at me, asking for help, in a way. He knows that I know he is a sicko like me.

"Maybe you need some alone time with her? Take her to the room right here." I point to the bedroom I see down the hallway with the door open, just off the dining room. "Stand up, whore."

She does it with tears flooding her eyes. "Get in the room, lie back on the bed and wait for him."

The boy tries to follow her in, but I stop him. "You listen to me, you try anything I won't put a bullet in you, I'll make it much more fun for me."

He nods.

"Now, get in there and make her scream. I want everyone out here to hear her."

"Leave it open." I tell him when he tries to close the door. "I'll be watching. No fun if I can't see it."

He looks at me a long moment before pulling his shirt over his head and going in for the girl, who is waiting on the edge of the bed for him. I smile a knowing grin at him. That girl is about to get the fuck of her life time in there.

I keep an eye on the remaining people in the dining room, but my real attention is drawn to what is going on in the bedroom, the light blue paint and sunflower border is a direct contradiction to what's about to happen to that woman on the bed in a minute.

The boy is inside of her already, wasting no time pushing her onto her knees and entering her slick hole from behind, pumping quickly; holding tightly to her hips and pushing into her hard.

She is soundless, though, not that she could be heard over the banging of the headboard or the squeak of the bed frame. Her face is vacant, the boy's ferociousness possibly scaring her.

"That's it, boy." I say to encourage him.

He seems to know what to do and thrusts deeper still. I cover my hard on with my hand and give it a good squeeze. This boy really knows what he wants. He is going at her like a madman. "You watch porn? You got some good shit going on there."

His grin tells me he appreciates the compliment.

"If you can't fuck her 'til she screams you better find a way to make her scream– we have an audience to impress."

He takes no time to understand what I mean, ripping her head up off the bed by her hair, making her yelp.

"Hit her." I grunt.

He puts his fist into her back, right at her kidney.

She screams.

"Nice." I say, massaging my cock. It's like watching porn, only better. I can practically smell the musky sex smell from here.

He does it again, then wraps both his fists into her hair and uses it like a rein to keep her in place as he forces himself inside her. I have a great side view of what he's doing to her. His eagerness is amazing.

She is squealing like a stuck pig now.

The others in the dining room are looking a little worried for her welfare, which only makes me enjoy this even more, he is savage.

And just when I think it can't get any better– or worse, depending on what side you're on– the kid fucking turns her face up toward him, looking her in the eyes then punches her right in the jaw. The crunch is louder than both the pounding and her screams that follow.

I can't believe it. I laugh before I can stop myself. "Fuck, boy, nice going. You got everyone in here worried for her. You got anything else in there for 'em?" The blood around her mouth is beautiful. If I wasn't on guard duty I'd go over and fuck it right now.

"What are you making him do to her?" I hear from Amy. Poor mom didn't know he'd be capable of something like this. I kind of feel sorry for her, shattering her illusion of her perfect little all-American blond haired boy.

I ignore her question, completely absorbed in what's happening with the woman and her wildly bouncing tits.

He seems to think about my question for a minute. Then, before I know what he's doing, he spits on her ass, and quicker than I've ever seen, he shoves his hard dick into that hole.

She looks ready to pass out from the abrupt and painful maneuver, losing her strength, her knees slide out from under her, leaving her sprawled out on the bedspread.

He barely misses a thrust, but he only lasts a few more before he grunts his own finish deep inside her torn ass.

Chapter Four

Travis

I can barely keep it together; I shove her forward until she is bent over the bed. "Get your knees up there, Kelly." She does and I get the perfect view of her meaty pussy. Chop was right, she is wet.

Maybe she is so used to being used by Stephen that her body responds to it now.

I slide my fingers through her slit and spread her open, ramming into her as hard as I can to fill her up. My first time in a pussy– so much better than I have ever imagined. And trust me, I have imagined– this in particular.

The closest I've come to fucking was watching an old babysitter get fucked by her boyfriend. I must be doing a good job, though, Chop has his hand on his crotch, much like I had mine while I jacked off watching that little slut get fucked. Or spread open while being eaten by her boyfriend countless times.

I fuck her at a pace that is hardly tapping into what I actually need right now. My excitement is boiling over.

I hear Chop say something, encouraging me to fuck harder, my dick plunging deeper, the cream in her pussy getting thick and making it easy to do.

"If you can't fuck her till she screams, you better make her scream…" Chop's words fade out as my ears are flooded with rushing blood.

I want to hurt her, I want to hear her scream, she's been silent up until now and I want so badly to hear her. And I do finally when I punch her in the kidney, knowing just the spot to make it hurt and piss blood for a week if done right. She clamps down on my cock as she reacts to the hit. So I do it again. I almost come right then, the grip so tight I have to fight against her to get moving again.

I want more, I want the screams back, not just the tears. So I grab her hair and just as our eyes meet I hit her right in the teeth. The feel of the pain radiate up my arm fuels my insides, mingling with the pleasure of her juicy pussy; so slick it is hard to get that beautiful friction back. This woman is so fucked up to be wet right now.

I do the only thing I know to do to build my friction, I spit onto her ass hole and use her own juices to double as lubrication to enter her ass. I do it hard, almost painful for my cock, but the pressure is there again and I fuck her hard until I come into her bloody asshole.

Chapter Five

Chop

She is openly crying now. Something that doesn't go unnoticed in the room full of people– his mother looking the most horrified of the bunch.

"Come on now, boy, get cleaned up." I grab his pants from the floor in front of the couch and toss them at him.

He pulls his pants over his hips after wiping his bloody cock off with the cream colored comforter. As he passes me in the doorway I tell him, "nice job, Travis." Clapping him on the sweaty shoulder the way a proud father might.

He hides his smile before joining the rest in the room.

His mother is looking at her son like he is a stranger, the things that went on in the room are not known to her, but there is no mistaking that it was horrible. She stays sitting instead of comforting him like a mother might want to do after her son had been forced to do those things in there. A part of her knowing he was possibly glad to accept the challenge.

The girl in the room is struggling to stand, her bloodied shaking legs unable to hold her weight. I do not let her get too far, spraying her brains on the wall behind her. The thwack of the gun startling everyone.

"She's better off dead after what happened in there, she'd never be the same after that." I laugh. She would definitely have some therapy bills, for sure.

There are sideways glances toward the boy, the questions of what actually happened in there written across their faces. They may be as scared of him as they are of me– maybe more so– I've only killed people.

Amy, his mother, seems to be taking it the hardest, probably devastated her son was capable of whatever made that bitch scream like that. Fuck, I'm a little shocked myself. Mom has got to be taking it hard.

Kinda like the dead girl– she took it pretty hard, too. I laugh at my own joke, confusing everyone not privy to my inner thoughts.

"Now that we've taken care of them, let's see here… you," I point to the mother of the two children. "What's your name?"

"Nancy."

"Ok, Nancy, it looks like you're up."

She pales and the excitement fills my insides.

"This is your husband?"

She nods slowly, hysterics building inside of her.

"You love him?"

"Very much." Her chin quivers, trying to hold back her tears.

"These his kids?"

Another nod, then the damn breaks and she loses it.

"Would you rather him die or one of the children?"

She takes a shaky breath between sobs. "Please, don't do this. You can just leave now and everything will be fine. Nothing…"

I cut her off, "That's not going to happen. Just answer the fucking question or I'll make you regret not."

She takes a long look through her tears, into her husband's eyes and just before she loses it again, he speaks up.

"It's ok, love, I know you have to protect the kids. I love you so much. I could never blame you for this choice he's forcing you to make."

She is crying again, sobbing. "I can't let you hurt my children," she says by way of an answer.

"Ok, great, then I'm going to need a few things." I turn away from her snotty, wet face.

"Boy, go find something– like a rope? Anything like that around here?"

He nods, "We have some in the garage. You want me to get 'em?"

I hear the eagerness to be helpful in his voice.

"You need me to threaten you with violence if you try anything stupid?" I don't really feel like I'd have to; this boy is the perfect assistant.

"Nah." And he leaves before I even can.

While he's gone I tell Nancy to place one of the dining chairs in the center of the room, underneath the exposed wooden ceiling beam. I take the rope from the boy, as he hands it over, and truss it up and around the beam, catching the end of it as it wraps snuggly around.

"Get over here, Dad." I say. "Up on the chair. You're wife made a decision that your life is less important than your children's, so, let's see if we can get her to follow through with that, shall we?"

"Nancy, come here." I tie the rope into a noose and place it around his neck.

He stares into my eyes, raging with hatred for me.

"Nancy, I'd like you to move the chair out from under him when I say. If you don't, I will kill one of your children." I drag her teenage son, by his throat, over to the scene and hold the gun steady to his head.

He is shaking under my hand.

"Do it now, Nancy."

She puts her hands on the chair back, but doesn't move it. "I'm so sorry, baby. I love you so much." She looks at me, begging. "Please don't make me do this, I could never live with this." She crumbles to her knees.

Before I can give her further instructions, her husband kicks the back of the chair, toppling it over and drops the few inches of slack before catching himself around the neck by the rope.

I roar and pull the trigger at his son's head. "I fucking told *her* to do that."

As his eyes see what he has done to his child with that decision, his legs kick frantically to find the chair and right himself, his fingers claw at his neck to get free of the rope.

"You did this, fucker." I kick the kid hard, with no response from him as the bullet killed him instantly.

A full minute later the man's hands slip from his neck, his shaking body stops– no more life left in him to fight. I watched as the light in his eyes dulled.

Keeping mine on his, so they'd be the last thing in this world that stupid fucker saw.

Nancy is crawling herself to her son, screams pouring from her lungs. I thought she was hysterical before– that was nothing compared to what the fuck is going on now. She is blubbering incoherent words to the dead men on the floor.

His sister pulls mom away, trying to calm her. They are holding tightly to each other, both knowing the other's pain.

"Come 'ere, girl. Your turn."

Nancy's red and tear streaked face pales, she hasn't had any time to properly mourn the rest of her family and she knows she's about to watch something horrific happen to her daughter, but she's too weak to do anything about it.

"Nooooooo," she whines.

I don't think I've enjoyed torturing a person quite like I'm enjoying this– her screams are like Viagra. She really knows how to make my efforts feel worth it.

The girl isn't standing up fast enough so I snatch her up. She stumbles twice before she can stay up on her feet– her mother grabbing hold of her ankles to keep her away from me. When she has control of her feet, she tries her best to act tough, setting her shoulders back and glaring at me.

"You know what happens in a strip club? All those hot young girls grinding against poles."

I love the look this her eyes. I can see a little of her reserve falter but she nods.

"Great, why don't you go show him a good time?" I point to Amy's man, Dan.

He stiffens, not knowing yet which of the two of them my target is.

"Get undressed," I tell him. "We got to make sure she's doing a good job."

"You're just going to shoot me anyway. So, fucking do it now and save everyone from this."

"That's not the way this works. I *want* to see it. Shooting you is the nicest way I could kill you. Do you want to hear about all the ways I could make you feel pain *before* killing you? All the things I've done in the past– that I dream about when I go to sleep, or the things I'm just aching to try. Do you like the thought of being my guinee pig? Do you want to see me *not* being nice?"

He begins to unbutton his polo shirt– really drawing out the time it takes him to get it done. "You got something wrong with your fingers that's making you move so fucking slowly? I'm not a very patient man, I'd hurry if I were you."

He picks up his pace, not quite as fast as he would normally go about it, but I let that slide.

He hesitates again when it comes to his underwear, stopping with his thumbs in his waistband, looking at me for permission to quit.

"I could lop your dick off if I don't see it in the next three seconds."

He sits back into the chair when he is sufficiently naked.

"Ok, girl, go show him a good time. Strip for him– for us. Make it sexy."

"I don't know how to do that." She says frantically.

"Move slow and take your clothes off– it's not too hard."

She starts to sway her hips side to side, walking closer to him.

He seems nervous and won't look at her.

"You're going to keep your eyes on her. All of you watch her– don't be rude."

Everyone's eyes go blankly to her. Travis eagerly watching now that her thin sweater has come off. *Good boy.*

"You liking this, Travis?"

His eyes are glued to her and without looking at me, he nods.

I smile. Watching his mom, Amy, look at him from the corner of her eyes, horrified.

"Everyone else having fun?" I don't get an answer, but then, I really don't expect one. This girl is *very* close to barely legal.

"Alright, girl, let's see those tits."

She moves her shaking hands behind her to unhook her bra– doing it unceremoniously. Her large-for- her- age tits bounce a little upon their release. Her nipples harden instantly.

I see something in Dan– he might actually be liking this. His cock is still soft, but we'll see what I can do about that.

"If you get hard you fuck her."

He looks at me shocked. "Chop, she's just a fuckin' kid."

"Then you better not get hard." I say it like he isn't already on his way to that right now.

He squeezes his eyes shut and reopens them with a new look of determination. I give him credit for trying, but I can see the fight raging in his eyes.

Just hearing the threat about forcing him to fuck her seems to have shaken him.

"You a virgin, girl?"

She looks at her mom over her shoulder, still lying in a heap on the floor, unable to bring herself to watch then nods her head in confirmation.

Whether it's true or not doesn't matter. That was the response I was hoping for, it brings a twitch to Dan's dick. He tries to cover it with his hand but I tell him to remove it.

"Don't be shy; you'll be doing much worse in a few minutes from the look of it." I say to him.

Amy, looking all the more horrified to learn her son was not the only monster in her midst.

"Amy, what do you think about your boy- toy fucking this hot little piece of ass?"

She snarls at me, making me chuckle. I can't wait for her turn.

"Why don't we get a look at your little ass now, girl? Take it all off."

Silent tears are running down her cheeks, she's no longer dancing. She does what she is told, pulling her skin- tight jeans down her legs, kicking out of both them and the panties I saw earlier for the briefest moment.

Hot pink.

Fuck.

"Grind your little pussy against him, let's see if he can hold back with that."

"Fucker!" he yells at me. Dan's semi- hard cock is growing now. He can't hide his excitement any longer.

"You sick pig." Amy hisses at him.

"Amy… I'm sorry. I don't want this, I promise. You know me, I'm not like this man. I don't know what it is– stress or something maybe? Oh, god, please," he begs to no one in particular.

"Why don't we just skip the grinding part, honey, his cock has made itself known."

"Quite the grower." I say as an aside to Dan.

"Why don't you just slip him inside of you on your way down to his lap?" I say to the girl.

She cries finally, looking at the massive cock she is up against. "I can't put that inside of me."

"Why don't you help her out? Get down there and make sure she's wet so it's not so scary for her."

He looks at me questioningly.

"With your mouth, idiot. Give her a little to get excited about."

He gets on his knees in front of her. "I'm so sorry, Lizzy," he says before spreading her open and positioning his upturned head between her thighs.

Her sobs are louder now.

"Put some fingers inside her. You're a big guy... do you want to tear her open?"

His grunt is muffled by her pussy; not pulling away to answer. It wasn't the grunt of a man who is not enjoying himself, it doesn't go unnoticed by the people in the room, particularly Lizzy who panics, pushing against his head.

He does what I say and pushes his fingers inside of her.

She yelps.

"You want to fuck her now?"

He doesn't answer, but sits back onto the floor. His mouth is glistening with saliva.

"Get her on it," I say.

He lays back, pulling her arms along with him, helping her situate herself into a straddle around his thighs. Grabbing the base of his cock, holding it in place as she settles against it.

I push her shoulders down until she is fully impaled

She squeals as his full length fills the inside of her.

"Lizzy, I'm gonna need you to make him happy. Why don't you do a little bouncing on his big dick?"

She does what her body will let her do while convulsing in hysterics, which is not as exciting as I need this to be.

"Help her out, she's new at this. Buck your fucking hips, mother fucker, the sooner you come the sooner it's over."

The slapping of her jiggling ass against his solid thighs is barely audible over her screams, his jack hammer approach to fucking her would do that to anyone.

He is grunting from the effort to keep this pace and just as I see signs of his finish I put a bullet in her head. She collapses onto his chest.

Instead of stopping, like a gentleman might, he gets more frantic, her convulsing body flopping about. He thrusts faster into her, gripping her hard around her waist to keep in her place, drawing out a moan for the duration of his pulsing cock emptying inside of her dead body.

"You fucker!" her mother yells, but not at me. She is on her feet and screaming at him. "You sick fucking pervert. Fucking her was one thing, being forced to do that, but you really had to fuck my little girl while she was dying? You sick piece of shit!" she has gotten so loud she's screeching.

She leaves the room, I let her only out of curiosity.

She comes back with a large knife from the kitchen and before the man can defend himself– still coming down from what I can only imagine was an awesome nut– and trapped by the full weight of Lizzy's dead body, she puts the knife into his eye socket.

He's not moving. I'm not sure if that worked to kill him, there's a lot of blood on the floor and the knife is buried to the hilt, so I have to assume he is. He died in what I can only imagine was the happiest state he's ever been.

I leave them attached by their crotches and move on, ripping the woman away from her victim.

"Well, now that it's just the four of us, and we're all a little worked up. Why don't we have a little fun together?"

I wait for everyone to become curious enough at my words to look at me.

"Travis, you want a go at her?" I point to the woman covered in the blood of her family members I've killed tonight– and the man she's taken it upon herself to do without help.

"Yea," he says, not hiding behind anymore masks of being a normal boy.

"Alright, but you fuck her you gotta kill her."

"You got it." He pulls the knife from the man's head, using two hands as it becomes clear it had been lodged into his skull.

He walks over to the table, setting the knife down as he undoes his pants and lets them fall to the floor. He drags Nancy to the spot her daughter's body was brutally raped and then killed– kicking Dan's arm aside, and hikes her skirt up over her ass, ripping her thong at the seam, effectively removing them.

Already hard, he pushes her face onto the table and enters her from behind.

The woman is all cried- out, however, his mother is in complete hysterics, becoming massively undone as he drags the knife across Nancy's throat and then fucks her dying body. Pulling her head back by the roots of her hair– it opens the gash in her neck and she gurgles around the sprays of arterial blood leaving her neck and spurting across the room.

She dies before he finishes and when he does he is laughing, fully lost in the sick nature of what he has just done.

Chapter Six

Travis

The thought of that, all the blood, much like the brutal underground porn I love to watch, excites me.

"You got it." I pull the knife from Dan's eye socket, which takes effort; that bitch stabbed him pretty good.

I drag Nancy to the table, letting my throbbing dick out of my pants. I lift her skirt over her ass and tear her underwear away. Her pussy is not wet like Kelly's– not as meaty either. I'm sure I'll still like it in here, but it may take a little something extra to really enjoy it. And as soon as the thought is in my head I know nothing else will work to get me off.

I fuck her hard until I'm sure how to go about it and then I drag the knife across her throat. And yeah, that fucking did it. Her pussy is in the middle of the most- extreme fight as her body writhes in the throes of her death.

I fuck her harder once she's dead, her body fitting me like a glove. Sweat pours from my forehead as I exert the last bit of energy to feed her pussy my come. Breathing hard, I collapse on her while I recover.

Chapter Seven

Chop

"Jesus, boy." I say, keeping a tight hold on his mother as she squirms against me.

"What? You didn't tell me what order I had to do it in." The boy has a fucking *smirk* on his face.

Oh, my fuck. This kid.

I wonder then, what it would be like. I've fucked my fair share of 'dead fish' women who just lie there while I fuck them. That was nothing like the excitement I got from watching Travis slice open her throat and fuck her.

"How was it?" I ask.

He walks over to me, dick still wet, and takes the gun I have pointed at his mother and puts a bullet right between her eyes. "Why don't you give it a try?"

Holy fuck.

I catch her body before it hits the floor and I do try it. I fuck her for longer than I've fucked anyone, coming inside of her pussy– and a moment later, when I'm hard again at the thought of her ass, I have a go at that, too.

Nothing had ever been that good. Although, I love the fight of a clawing and scratching woman I'm fucking– this is something different. All my effort could go into the fucking– not having the struggle deplete my energy. I pounded relentlessly into her body. Growling like a fucking animal with all the power.

Travis watching has him interested in his girl again, and he gets another round in with her.

We fuck them until absolutely and utterly spent– the both of us.

After getting dressed, while I'm still wondering what to do with this boy he answers my unasked question. "Where to now, Chop?"

Seems I've got a hunting buddy now and the boy is full of great ideas, but I have a few that could change his life, too.

I plan on taking him to meet Jamie, the girl Gabe was asking about tonight. The play- thing I've been enjoying in my basement for the last week. "I got just the girl for us."

He looks excited, even after all we've done here tonight; he could probably give Jamie a few good rounds when we get home. Maybe we could have a go at her together? One on either end like a pig on a spit.

"Grab some shit, boy, I got just the place.

The End

Thank you for taking the time to read. I hope you enjoyed.

Let me know what you thought by leaving a review

Made in the USA
Monee, IL
11 October 2023

44373859R00049